CUMBRIA LIBRARIES

KT-151-658

3 8003 04816 8504

Dirty Bertie

DISCO!

For Nathaniel ~ D R
For Reece Coggan and Tyra Barnes –
thanks for the great story ideas! ~ A M

STRIPES PUBLISHING
An imprint of the Little Tiger Group
1 The Coda Centre, 189 Munster Road,
London SW6 6AW

A paperback original
First published in Great Britain in 2017

Characters created by David Roberts
Text copyright © Alan MacDonald, 2017
Illustrations copyright © David Roberts, 2017

ISBN: 978-1-84715-781-2

The right of Alan MacDonald and David Roberts to
be identified as the author and illustrator of this work
respectively has been asserted by them in accordance
with the Copyright, Designs and Patents Act, 1988.

All rights reserved.

A CIP catalogue record for this book is available from
the British Library.

This book is sold subject to the condition that it shall not,
by way of trade or otherwise, be lent, resold, hired out, or
otherwise circulated without the publisher's prior consent
in any form of binding or cover other than that in which it
is published and without a similar condition including this
condition being imposed upon the subsequent purchaser.

Printed and bound in the UK.

10 9 8 7 6 5 4 3 2 1

Dirty Bertie

DISCO!

DAVID ROBERTS WRITTEN BY ALAN MACDONALD

stripes

Collect all the Dirty Bertie books!

Contents

DISCO!

CHAPTER 1

Bertie's head flopped forwards. It was Monday assembly and as usual Miss Skinner had been droning on for hours.

"Now," she said. "Listen carefully because Miss Darling has some exciting news."

Miss Darling stood up. "As you know we're nearing the end of term," she said.

Dirty Bertie

"And this year we are holding our very first Pudsley Prom Party!"

Bertie looked up. *What?* A Prom Party? But they always watched a film at the end of the summer term. It was the one thing he looked forward to every year!

"It's going to be heaps of fun," said Miss Darling. "There will be party food and games and prizes. And of course, you can't have a prom without dancing."

Bertie groaned. *Dancing?* YUCK! It sounded like torture! Why couldn't they watch *The Blob from Planet Zog* like last year?

After assembly he trailed back to class with his friends.

Dirty Bertie

"A Prom Party?" he grumbled. "Who wants to go to a stupid prom?"

"Lots of schools have them," said Eugene.

"My cousin arrived at his prom in a massive stretch limo," said Darren.

"Really?" said Bertie.

He wouldn't mind arriving in a limo, as long as he could choose who came in it. Obviously Know-All Nick could walk. But even so, it wouldn't make the prom any more bearable.

"Why's there got to be dancing?" he complained.

Bertie hated dancing. He always trod on people's feet. His mum had once dragged him along to his sister's dance class. Miss Foxtrot had made him wear ballet shoes and prance up and down on tippy toes. He wouldn't be doing that again in a hurry.

"It'll be just like a school disco," said Eugene. "I like dancing."

"Well, I don't," said Bertie. "And I'm not dancing with any girls! No way!"

Darren smiled and glanced at Eugene. "It's a prom, Bertie," he said. "Surely you know about proms?"

Bertie frowned. "Know what?"

"That you *have* to take a girl," said Darren. "Isn't that right, Eugene?"

"Do you?" Eugene gulped. It was news to him.

Darren winked. "Course you do!" he said. "That's the whole point."

Bertie had turned deathly white. Surely they couldn't be serious?

"TAKE A GIRL?" he said, almost choking. "You mean like — you go *together*?"

"Yes," said Darren. "But obviously you have to ask them first."

"ASK THEM?" said Bertie.

"Of course," said Darren. "You'll need a partner or you won't have anyone to dance with! So who are you going to ask?"

Bertie looked as if he might pass out. How could Miss Darling do this to him? She actually expected him to ask a girl to the prom and then dance with her? It was too horrible for words! He felt sick just thinking about it.

"No, no, I can't," he muttered, shaking his head. "I'm not doing it!"

Darren shrugged. "Please yourself, but you'll miss all the games and prizes — and the party food. And you know what they'll make you do if you don't go to the prom?"

"What?" asked Bertie.

"Extra maths with Miss Boot," said Darren.

Bertie stared in disbelief. "Wait a minute," he said. "If we've ALL got to ask a girl, then you'll have to do it, too."

Dirty Bertie

"Of course!" said Darren. "We don't mind, do we, Eugene?"

"Erm … no, no problem," said Eugene doubtfully.

Bertie's shoulders drooped. He ducked into the toilets saying he didn't feel well.

Dirty Bertie

Eugene turned to Darren. "Are you serious?" he moaned. "We *really* have to take a *girl*?"

Darren laughed. "Course we don't!" he said. "I only made it up because I knew Bertie would be terrified! I can't believe he actually fell for it."

"You had me worried for a minute there," said Eugene. "But shouldn't we tell him the truth?"

"Are you kidding?" said Darren. "This could be the best joke ever. Imagine Bertie turning up to the prom with a girl. It'll be hilarious!"

CHAPTER 2

For the rest of the day Bertie went around under a dark cloud. How could his classmates carry on as if everything was normal? He needed advice but who could he ask? His friends weren't worried about the prom and his parents would say he was making a fuss about nothing. What about his sister, Suzy?

Dirty Bertie

As soon as he got home, he raced upstairs to her room.

"What do you want?" groaned Suzy.

"I suppose you've heard about this Prom Party?" Bertie said.

"Oh yes, for you younger kids," said Suzy. "Sounds fun."

"Fun!" cried Bertie. "I've just found out we have to bring someone."

Suzy looked puzzled. "Who?"

"A girl!" said Bertie. "You've got to bring a girl or you can't go!"

Suzy raised her eyebrows. "And who told you that?" she asked.

"Darren," said Bertie. "Why? Isn't it true?"

Suzy smiled. It was obvious Bertie's friends were playing a joke on him. Of course she could easily put him out of his misery... On the other hand, this was her bogey-nosed, annoying little brother. It was much funnier to play along.

"Of course it's true," she said. "Everyone takes a partner to a prom."

Bertie sank down on the bed in despair. So Darren was right!

"But I CAN'T! Who can I ask?" he moaned.

"What about the girls in your class?" asked Suzy.

"But they're all … GIRLS!" said Bertie. "I can't ask them!"

Suzy smiled. "Come on, there must be one you like," she teased.

"SHUT UP! THERE ISN'T!" wailed Bertie.

"It's only a dance," said Suzy, trying not to laugh. "You don't have to marry them!"

Bertie shuddered. He'd never danced with a girl in his life – except for the time Miss Boot forced him to try country dancing, and then he'd kept his eyes closed.

Dirty Bertie

"You've got to help me!" he begged. "What can I do?"

Suzy folded her arms. "It's easy. You've got two choices," she said. "Either you miss the prom altogether ... or you find a girl to go with you."

Bertie buried his head in his hands. It was too horrible! But if he missed the prom, he'd be stuck in a room with Miss Boot doing extra maths – a fate worse than dancing!

CHAPTER 3

Friday, the dreaded day of the Prom Party, arrived. Bertie trailed down to breakfast.

"I'm feeling a bit sick," he croaked, pushing his cereal around his bowl.

"Nonsense, it's your Prom Party today," said Mum.

"I don't think I can go," moaned

Bertie. "I've got feet ache!"

Mum sighed. "Toothache, tummy ache, I've heard it all before, Bertie," she said. "You're going to school and that's the end of it."

Darren and Eugene were waiting for Bertie in the playground.

"Well?" asked Darren. "Have you found someone to take to the prom?"

Bertie shook his head.

"You better get a move on – it's this afternoon," said Eugene.

"Yes, we've asked our partners," boasted Darren.

"Seriously? WHO?" said Bertie.

Darren quickly looked around. Two girls were just entering the school gates.

"Them," said Darren.

"Pamela and Amanda?" said Bertie. "How did you manage it?"

"Oh, it was easy," shrugged Darren. "Wasn't it, Eugene?"

"Yes," agreed Eugene. "We just went straight up and asked them."

Bertie stared. Darren had never shown any interest in Pamela or Amanda before. And he couldn't remember Eugene ever actually speaking to a girl! All the same, if they both had prom partners he couldn't put it off any longer.

"What about Donna?" said Darren.

"Donna?" squeaked Bertie.

"Yes, I bet she'd go to the prom with you," said Eugene. "She likes you."

Bertie looked over at Donna, who was sitting on a wall waiting for her friends. He didn't mind Donna – she was clever and she knew a lot about dogs. But as for asking her to the prom – he'd rather ask a frog.

"Go on!" urged Darren. "While she's by herself."

Bertie took a deep breath and plodded over. His hands were sweating and his throat was dry.

"Hi, Donna," he mumbled.

"Oh, hi, Bertie!" said Donna. "Okay?"

"Yes … fine, great, good," said Bertie. He hummed tunelessly and looked at the sky. His legs had started to tremble.

"Did you want something?" asked Donna.

"Me?"

"Yes, you looked like you wanted to say something," said Donna, frowning.

Just come straight out and ask her, thought Bertie. He cleared his throat.

"I was, um … wondering … if well…"

"Yes?" said Donna.

"If … um … you … if you still have a dog?" stammered Bertie.

Dirty Bertie

"Cookie? Yes, I've still got him," replied Donna.

"Ah," said Bertie. "That's good. Well, bye then!"

He fled back to his friends.

"Did you ask her?" asked Eugene.

"Yes," said Bertie. "She's still got a dog."

The morning sped by without Bertie having any success. Darren and Eugene suggested four or five girls in their class but Bertie's nerve failed him every time. His mouth turned dry and his mind went blank as soon as he got near them. Once he tried passing a note to Kelly, which said:

WILL YOO CUME TO THE PROM?

But the note only reached Know-All Nick, who thought it was a joke and threw it back at Bertie. Time was running out. The prom was due to start at two o'clock – and Bertie still didn't have a partner.

"It's no use!" he sighed as he trailed outside at break. "I'll just have to go on my own."

"You can't" said Darren quickly. "They won't let you in."

"Won't they?"

"No, it's a prom!" said Darren. "They'll send you to Miss Boot."

"Anyway, you can't dance by yourself," argued Eugene.

Bertie didn't want to dance at all. He just wanted to sit watching a film like they always did.

Dirty Bertie

DONK! Suddenly a tennis ball hit him on the head.

Bertie picked it up. Angela Nicely came running over. Angela lived next door and had been in love with Bertie forever.

"Sorry, Bertie!" she giggled. "Are you okay?"

A thought crept into Bertie's head. Normally he avoided Angela like a cold bath but this was an emergency. He had to find someone to take to the prom and she was his only chance. He took a deep breath.

"Listen," he mumbled. "Do you, er ... want to go to this prom thing?"

"I *am* going!" trilled Angela. "We're all going!"

"Yes, but I mean go with me," said Bertie, turning red.

Angela blinked. "With you? You mean go *together*?" she said.

Bertie gulped and nodded.

"Yee-hoo!" cried Angela. "Wait till I tell Laura and Maisie!"

She hugged him and ran off.

Bertie watched her go. What had he done? A Prom Party with adoring Angela sticking to him like glue. This was going to be the worst day of his life!

CHAPTER 4

At two o'clock, Bertie stood nervously outside the hall waiting for Angela. His suit itched and his bow tie was too tight. Inside he could hear loud music. The Prom Party was already in full swing.

Darren and Eugene arrived.

"So where is she?" asked Darren. "This mystery girlfriend of yours?"

"She's not my girlfriend," scowled Bertie. "It's just for the prom. Anyway, where are Pamela and Amanda?"

"Who?" said Eugene.

"Oh, they're meeting us inside," said Darren.

"Hi, Bertie!" squeaked an excited voice.

Darren and Eugene stared. Angela was wearing her frilly party dress with pink sparkly shoes and a new bow in her hair.

"Angela? *She's* your girlfriend?" hooted Darren.

"She's NOT my girlfriend!" groaned Bertie.

"You said!" pouted Angela. "You said you wanted to go together!"

"I do," said Bertie quickly. "But it's just for the prom, okay?"

Angela stuck out her bottom lip.

"Well if you're going to be mean…"
she said sulkily.

"Sorry," Bertie muttered. "Let's go in."

Angela brightened up and held out
her hand.

Bertie sighed and took it. This was
worse than the time he'd turned up for
swimming without his trunks.

"After you!" grinned Darren, holding
open the door.

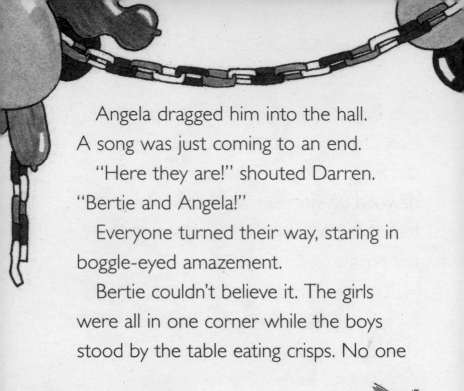

Angela dragged him into the hall.
A song was just coming to an end.

"Here they are!" shouted Darren.
"Bertie and Angela!"

Everyone turned their way, staring in
boggle-eyed amazement.

Bertie couldn't believe it. The girls
were all in one corner while the boys
stood by the table eating crisps. No one

was dancing or holding hands, apart from him. Darren and Eugene were giggling like a pair of idiots. The horrible truth dawned on Bertie. It was all a rotten trick. No one else had brought a girl to the prom.

"Your face! Hee hee!" hooted Darren.

"Ha ha! You actually fell for it!" chuckled Eugene.

Bertie dropped Angela's hand.

"Come on, Bertie, let's dance," she cried as the music started. "Oh, but what about your friends? They don't have anyone to dance with."

Bertie smiled. "Oh dear, that's no good," he said. "What shall we do?"

"I know," cried Angela. "Wait there! I'll get Maisie and Laura!"

Darren and Eugene looked horrified.

"No, no ... don't!" stammered Darren.

"We're fine," gulped Eugene.

But it was too late. Angela was already running over, towing her two friends behind her. Darren and Eugene backed away but Bertie made sure they didn't escape.

"Oh no," he said, "you can't come to

a Prom Party without a partner! And anyway, I thought you *liked* dancing?"

CHAPTER 1

It was Wednesday afternoon and Gran had dropped in for tea, which always meant they had cake. Bertie reached out to grab the biggest slice.

"Bertie!" groaned Mum. "Guests first, please!"

"Have shum cake, Gran," said Bertie with his mouth full.

Dirty Bertie

"Sorry, Gran," sighed Mum. "What were you saying?"

"This Saturday," said Gran. "It's the Sunset Club's annual coach trip. We're going to Skegby-on-Sea."

"That'll be nice," said Mum.

"Yes," said Gran. "A few people have dropped out, so I did wonder if Bertie might like to come?"

"ME? WHERE?" asked Bertie, spraying cake crumbs everywhere.

Gran dusted off the front of her dress with a tissue.

"On a day trip to Skegby," she said.

"It's at the seaside," added Mum.

Dirty Bertie

The seaside? Bertie's eyes lit up. He hadn't been to the seaside in years – at least since last summer. Hang on, though, he'd learned to be careful when Gran was handing out invitations. The last time she offered to take him to the cinema her new boyfriend, Reg, had come along. Bertie had been forced to spill his Strawberry Slushy in Reg's lap to stop them kissing!

"Who's going?" he asked suspiciously.

"I told you – my friends from the Sunset Club," replied Gran. "You remember Sherry?"

Bertie could hardly forget her – when Sherry and Gran got together they were like a pair of naughty schoolgirls. Sherry wore bright red lipstick and giggled a lot.

"Is everyone going to be *old*?" asked Bertie.

"No, mostly my age," answered Gran.

Dirty Bertie

"You mean a hundred?" said Bertie.

"*Sixty-seven*, if you don't mind," huffed Gran. "But don't let me force you, Bertie, I just thought it would be a treat."

"It sounds fun," said Mum, seeing the chance of a Bertie-free day. "You could build sandcastles on the beach, maybe even paddle in the sea."

Bertie considered it. "Are any other children going?" he asked.

"I doubt it," said Gran, "but it's always a great day out. Our tour guide Gerry's a scream. We play bingo and crazy golf and sing songs all the way home."

Bertie frowned. He'd heard Gran's singing and she sounded like she was in pain. Imagine fifty or more grannies warbling away on a coach! He'd have to take earplugs. All the same, it *was* a trip

to the seaside and the best part was
that Gran always paid for everything.

"Of course it's up to you," said Mum,
pouring more tea. "But I'm pretty sure
Skegby has a funfair."

"A FUNFAIR!" cried Bertie.

That settled it, he was definitely going.

CHAPTER 2

On Saturday morning Dad dropped
them in town at the coach pick-up
point. Bertie had brought everything he
needed for the day – swimming trunks,
towel, rubber ring, bucket and spade,
plus enough sweets to last a month.

"Are you sure you're going to need all
that?" Gran asked.

"I always bring this stuff to the
seaside," replied Bertie.

He looked around at the crowd
waiting to board the coach. Everyone
seemed to be ancient.

"They're even older than you, Gran,"
he said.

"SHH! Not so loud!" hissed Gran.

Sherry spotted them and came
bustling over.

"Hello, Dotty," she cooed. "And I've
met this handsome young man before.
Are you sitting next to me, Bertie?
Hee hee!"

Bertie shrank back as Sherry planted
a big sloppy kiss on his cheek. He hoped
it wasn't going to be like this all day. If
everyone wanted to kiss him, he'd have
to wear a bucket over his head.

"Right, are we all here?" asked a loud voice.

A tall, prim woman holding a clipboard stood at the coach door. She had a beaky nose and a stern expression.

"Who's that?" asked Gran. "Where's Gerry?"

"Oh, didn't you hear? He's poorly," sighed Sherry. "They've sent us this one, instead – her name's Miss Stickler."

Dirty Bertie

Gran stared in dismay. "But Gerry always takes us to Skegby," she said. "He's the reason it's so much fun!"

Bertie didn't think Miss Stickler looked like she'd heard of fun. She was making everyone form an orderly line as if they were back at school.

"Goodness – who's this?" she asked, when she saw Bertie.

"This is my grandson Bertie," explained Gran.

"Isn't he a bit young for the Sunset Club?" said Miss Stickler. "I hope he's going to behave himself."

"Of course he is," said Gran. "Bertie's never any trouble, are you, Bertie?"

"No," said Bertie, which was partly true. He never *meant* to be any trouble, it was just that trouble had a habit of following him around.

The coach set off. To Bertie's relief, Gran sat down beside him while Sherry took a seat with a chap called Ted. Once they were on the motorway, Miss Stickler stood up.

"Good morning and welcome," she said. "As you may know, Gerry has lost his voice and sadly can't be with us. But the good news is – I'm going to be your tour guide for the day. I have drawn up a timetable of activities and I'm sure we'll all have a wonderful day. Are there any questions?"

Bertie raised his hand. "When do we go to the funfair?" he asked.

Miss Stickler pulled a face. "I hardly think anyone wants to visit the *funfair*," she sniffed. "In any case, it's not on my timetable."

Bertie blinked. *Not go to the funfair?* But that was the whole point of coming!

Gran patted his hand. "Don't worry, Bertie," she whispered. "I'm sure we can pop along there at some point."

CHAPTER 3

At last the coach arrived at Skegby-on-Sea. Bertie and Gran waited to get off. It had been a long journey with about a hundred stops for the toilet. Miss Stickler had spent the whole time telling Bertie off – for kicking the seat in front, dropping sweet wrappers and making rude noises with his rubber ring.

Dirty Bertie

As they got out, Miss Stickler handed everyone a printed sheet.

"What's this?" asked Gran.

"Our timetable for today," replied Miss Stickler. "There's one each so that everyone's clear what we're doing and at what time."

Bertie read down the list. There were visits to tea shops, an antiques market, a church and the Skegby Pencil Museum. There was no mention of paddling, sandcastles or going anywhere near the funfair.

"It's the seaside!" Bertie grumbled. "We have to go to the beach."

"It's far too windy," said Miss Stickler. "I don't want anyone catching a cold."

"We could play football," suggested Bertie. "That would warm us up!"

Dirty Bertie

"This is a trip for the elderly," sniffed Miss Stickler. "I think you'll find my programme has something for everyone."

"Not for me," muttered Gran. "Where's the bingo?"

"And the crazy golf?" added Sherry.

"Gerry always takes us to the pier," grumbled Ted loudly.

Dirty Bertie

"Well, Gerry isn't here," snapped Miss Stickler. "I think you'll find the Pencil Museum is really quite exciting. Now follow me, please, and try to keep up."

She set off, marching down the road with her umbrella held high.

Gran shook her head. "You can go off people," she muttered.

Dirty Bertie

"I didn't like her from the start," said Sherry.

Bertie trailed along with Gran, wearing his rubber ring and dragging his bucket and spade. He stared longingly at the beach, where a few children were playing on the sand.

"Can't I stay here?" he moaned.

"Sorry, Bertie," sighed Gran. "I promised your mum I wouldn't let you out of my sight. Maybe we'll have time for the beach or the funfair later?"

But Miss Stickler had other ideas. She marched them from one boring place to the next. The Pencil Museum had a thrilling display of 300 pencils, while the antiques market had endless stalls selling piles of old junk. As they walked along the seafront, Bertie could see the bright lights of the funfair and hear the occasional snatch of music. It was torture being so close.

"Mum promised me the funfair!" he grumbled.

"Believe me, I'd love to go," sighed Gran. "But it's not on the blooming timetable."

Dirty Bertie

Later that afternoon they made their second tea stop. Bertie looked around the café gloomily. Ted seemed to have nodded off while the rest of the party looked dead on their feet. The coach was due to leave at five, which meant they had less than two hours.

"Can't we go to the funfair *now*?" Bertie begged Gran.

Gran sighed. "I'm sorry, Bertie, I've told you — I'm not in charge."

"Pity," sighed Sherry. "I do love a good funfair!"

Ted suddenly sat up and opened his eyes. "A funfair? I haven't been to one of those in years!" he cried.

Bertie glanced over at Miss Stickler, who was nibbling a teacake. If she wouldn't take them then they'd just have to find another way.

"Why don't we escape?" he whispered.

"ESCAPE?" asked Gran.

"Yes," said Bertie. "If we can give her the slip, what's to stop us? We can all go."

Gran and Sherry looked at each other.

"How exciting!" giggled Sherry. "It'll be like one of those films where they break out of prison."

"Do we have to dig a tunnel?" asked Ted.

Bertie shook his head. "No. We just need old Sticklepants out of the way for five minutes."

He explained his plan while the other three listened, nodding their heads. The Great Escape was on, but they'd have to move fast. Smuggling fifty pensioners out of a teashop right under Miss Stickler's nose wasn't going to be easy!

CHAPTER 4

"Oh dear! Oh no! Where can it be?" wailed Gran, her head in her hands.

Bertie thought that she was overacting but it did the trick – Miss Stickler was coming over.

"What's the matter?" she demanded.

"I can't find my purse," said Gran.

"Well, where did you last have it?"

asked Miss Stickler.

"Um, let me think … in the toilets … yes, that was it," said Gran.

Miss Stickler sighed. Old people were always losing things. If it wasn't money, it was their keys or their false teeth.

Gran led the way to the Ladies toilets and opened the door.

"After you," she said politely.

Miss Stickler went in. There was no sign of the purse by the basins. She opened a cubicle door and looked on the floor.

"Are you sure you—?"

WHAM!

Suddenly the door to the Ladies toilets slammed shut. Miss Stickler stared round in surprise.

"HEY! WHAT'S GOING ON?" she

cried, trying the door handle. It refused to open.

Outside, Bertie helped Gran to wedge the door shut with a chair.

"Quick!" said Bertie. "Let's go before she gets out!"

Gran and Sherry rounded up the rest of the party, which wasn't easy. Some of them protested they hadn't finished their tea.

"Sorry, there isn't time," said Gran, glancing at the toilets. "Please do hurry!"

THUMP! THUMP!

"LET ME OUT!" yelled Miss Stickler, banging on the door.

"Come *on!*" urged Bertie, herding the group out of the café. "Head for the funfair. It's time we enjoyed ourselves!"

"The bus fare?" said one lady. "I thought we came by coach!"

THUD! THUD! CRASH!

The door to the Ladies toilets finally burst open and Miss Stickler stumbled out. She was astonished to find the café deserted. Toasted teacakes sat on plates half eaten, with the tea still warm in the cups.

A waitress appeared holding a tray.

"Where did they all go?" demanded Miss Stickler. "The old people!"

"I've no idea," replied the waitress. "They just got up and left all of a sudden. But someone will have to pay the bill."

Miss Stickler glared and fished out her purse. She had a pretty good idea who was behind this.

Dirty Bertie

"Wheee! Hold tight, Bertie!" squealed Gran.

Bertie hung on as the big wheel took them round again. The funfair had proved a big hit with the Sunset Club. Many of them said they hadn't had such a great time in years. They'd whooped on the dodgems, screamed on the ghost train and had to sit down after getting dizzy on the merry-go-round.

"That was a hoot!" giggled Sherry, as the big wheel came to a stop. "What shall we do next?"

Dirty Bertie

Bertie lifted the safety barrier and climbed out. His face fell. A tall, stern woman was marching towards them.

"STOP RIGHT THERE!" shouted Miss Stickler. "I knew you were behind all this."

Bertie gulped. Miss Stickler's face was bright red. She looked like she'd run a marathon.

"How *dare* you?" she stormed. "Locking me in the toilets. I've had to chase all over town looking for you!"

"Oh dear!" said Gran. "You poor thing. You'd better sit down."

Gran nudged Bertie, who took a moment to catch on.

"Yes, have a seat," said Bertie, taking Miss Stickler's arm.

He helped her into a padded seat, framed by coloured lights.

"You should be ashamed," Miss Stickler panted. "Behaving like schoolkids."

"I am a schoolkid," replied Bertie. "Now hold on tight."

"What?" asked Miss Stickler, confused.

CLUNK!

The safety barrier came down over her head and music began to play.

Miss Stickler looked around in panic. Her seat was slowly rising off the ground. She was on the big wheel and it was taking her up!

"HEEEELP!" she squawked. "GET ME DOWN!"

"Bye, bye, Miss Stickler!" cried Bertie, waving from below.

"Well, that ought to keep her busy for a while," smiled Gran. "So what's next then, Bertie?"

"The helter skelter!" cried Bertie. "Come on, I'll race you!"

CHAPTER 1

Bertie had seen the worm farm in a shop
window when he was passing with his
mum. He could hardly believe his eyes.
Who needed sheep and cows when you
could own a farm with real live worms?
He'd decided there and then he had to
have it.

Bertie loved worms and they made

the perfect pets. He still hadn't forgotten Arthur, his pet worm who'd lived in his bedroom until Mum discovered him. But a worm farm was even better – you got a whole family of worms for just £9.99!

The only problem was, Bertie didn't have £9.99. He'd spent all his pocket money on sweets and it was no good asking his family to help. Dad said worms belonged in the garden, Mum thought they were revolting, while Gran screamed if she came near one.

On the way to school, Bertie asked his friends to help.

"Ten pounds? For a bunch of worms?" said Darren. "You must be joking!"

"It's a worm farm," explained Bertie. "You can watch them squirming about."

Dirty Bertie

"Yuck!" said Darren. "Anyway, I haven't got ten pounds."

Bertie sighed. "What about you, Eugene?"

"I'm not that keen on worms," said Eugene.

"Yes, but can you lend me ten pounds?" said Bertie.

Eugene shook his head. "Sorry, Bertie, I'm saving up for a new violin case."

Bertie rolled his eyes. So much for friends! Didn't they know how important this was? It might be his one and only chance to own a worm farm!

There had to be someone who would lend him ten pounds. It was no use asking Know-All Nick – he wouldn't lend Bertie a used hanky. But what about Royston Rich? He had pots of money! He was always boasting that his dad was practically a millionaire.

There was just one snag – Royston and Bertie weren't friends. Royston had never forgiven him for ruining his swimming party when Whiffer left a present in his pool.

Still, it was worth a try – Royston was probably the one person in his class who actually HAD ten pounds.

Dirty Bertie

At school Bertie tracked down Royston in the playground.

"Hi, Royston, old pal," said Bertie.

"What do *you* want?" Royston scowled.

"Nothing," said Bertie. "Only, I was just wondering – how much pocket money do you get a week?"

"Loads more than you," boasted Royston.

"Great," said Bertie. "In that case, could you lend me ten pounds?"

Dirty Bertie

"TEN POUNDS?" cried Royston.

"Yes, to buy a worm farm," explained Bertie. "I'll pay you back."

"No chance!" snorted Royston. "I wouldn't lend you ten pounds if you got down on your knees and begged!" A sly look crossed his face. "But if you REALLY want the money…" he said.

"I'll do anything," said Bertie.

Dirty Bertie

"Okay then, what if I pay you ten pounds – to be my slave for the day?" said Royston.

Bertie gulped. "W-what?"

"You heard me," said Royston. He pulled out a ten pound note from his pocket and waved it in the air.

"Uh-uh," he said, as Bertie reached out. "You have to earn it first. Do we have a deal?"

Bertie thought fast. He couldn't imagine anything worse than being Royston's slave. He'd rather marry Angela Nicely! On the other hand, it'd take him years to save up enough pocket money to buy the worm farm himself.

"Okay, it's a deal," he said.

Royston gave a goofy grin as he shook Bertie's hand.

"Super!" he said. "Of course my slave has to do anything I want – all day."

"Just until the end of school," said Bertie.

"Let's say four o'clock," said Royston.

He rubbed his hands with glee. He'd always wanted his own slave. Bertie had no idea what he'd let himself in for!

CHAPTER 2

"What was all that about?" asked Eugene when Bertie returned.

"I've just agreed to be Royston's slave," said Bertie.

"Are you MAD?" asked Darren.

Bertie shrugged. "He's paying me ten pounds."

"Yes, but you have to be his slave!"

"Only for today," said Bertie.

"You wouldn't catch me being Royston's slave!" said Darren. "You know what he's like."

Bertie knew only too well. Royston was born ordering people around. He probably had servants at home to fold his clothes, do his homework and brush his teeth.

"It can't be that bad," said Bertie.

"I wouldn't bet on it," said Eugene. "He'll probably treat you like dirt."

"OH SLAVE!" sang a voice. "Where has my slave got to?"

Darren raised his eyebrows. "Better not keep his lordship waiting," he said.

Bertie trailed over.

"Where were you?" demanded Royston.

"With my friends," answered Bertie.

"I didn't give you time off," said Royston. "And call me 'master' or 'your highness'."

Bertie frowned. He could think of a lot of other things to call Royston.

"What do you want then, *master?*" he asked.

"And bow when you're speaking to me," said Royston.

Bertie glared. This was pushing things too far. He ducked his head, hoping that no one was watching.

"My shoes are dirty," said Royston.

"They look fine to me," said Bertie.

"If I say they're dirty, then they're dirty," said Royston. And to prove his point, he stepped in a big muddy puddle.

"Clean them, slave," he ordered.

Bertie gaped. "What with?"

"That's your problem," said Royston. "When I give you an order, I expect you to do it – and I told you to call me master."

Bertie was about to tell Royston to clean his own stupid shoes – but slaves weren't allowed to answer back. He kneeled down and wiped Royston's

Dirty Bertie

shoes with a grubby tissue.

"There, all done," he said.

Royston folded his arms. "I want them polished, slave," he said. "I want to see my face in them."

Bertie got back on his knees. Luckily, just at that moment, the bell rang. For once Bertie couldn't wait to go into school. At least Royston wouldn't be able to order him around in class.

CHAPTER 3

"Hurry up and sit down!" barked Miss Boot.

Bertie went to take his usual seat with his friends.

"Not there, slave!" said Royston. "You're sitting next to me."

"But that's my seat, I always sit there," protested Bertie.

Dirty Bertie

"Not today," said Royston. "You sit where you're told."

"BERTIE!" thundered Miss Boot. "Why are you still wandering around? Find a seat!"

Bertie slumped into the chair beside Royston. He'd been hoping to get away from him in lessons. Still, he just had to stick it out until four o'clock, then he'd have ten whole pounds to spend.

Miss Boot went round, handing out worksheets.

"We'll begin with a maths test," she said. "You have thirty minutes to finish. And I expect you all to work in total silence."

Bertie groaned. He hated maths tests – the questions made his brain hurt. They were always about Peter, Susan and Nadia, who had eight sweets and added four and then took away three. Why couldn't they just get on and eat them?

"Slave!" Royston hissed in his ear.

Bertie groaned. "What now?"

"What now, master?" Royston insisted.

"I'm trying to work!" said Bertie.

Royston slid his test paper across the desk.

"You can do mine," he said. "I'm too tired to think about maths today."

"WHAT? I can't!" argued Bertie.

"Of course you can, that's what slaves are for," said Royston.

Bertie glanced up at Miss Boot, who had her eye on the class.

"We'll get caught!" he whispered.

Dirty Bertie

"Then I'll say *you* were copying *me*," said Royston. "Hurry up – and make sure you get a better mark than last time."

Royston sat back in his seat. Bertie couldn't believe it! How was he meant to do Royston's test as well as his own? He had a good mind to chuck Royston's paper in the bin. But that would put an end to their deal. He'd just have to work at double speed.

Dirty Bertie

As the clock ticked, Bertie scribbled answers on Royston's test paper, writing down the first thing that came into his head. If Royston came bottom of the class, that was his own fault, he thought. Finally he completed the last question – now to start on his own paper…

"Right, everyone put down your pens!" boomed Miss Boot. "Who has completed all the questions?"

A few hands went up – one of them was Royston's.

"I have, Miss Boot!" he smirked.

"Excellent, Royston, and what about you, Bertie?" asked Miss Boot.

"Um, I made a start…" mumbled Bertie.

"Let me see," said Miss Boot marching over.

"All you've written is your name!" she snapped. "Idling as usual! You can have extra maths homework tonight."

Bertie glared at Royston, who wagged his finger and tutted.

"Oh dear, Bertie!" he jeered. "You never learn, do you?"

CHAPTER 4

Bertie slaved for Royston all morning.
At lunch Royston wanted his slave to
wait on him at the table. Bertie was
kept running back and forth to fetch
salt, ketchup, napkins and a clean spoon.
When he finally sat down to eat, his
food had gone stone cold.

During the afternoon it poured with

rain. Royston demanded to be sheltered under an umbrella while Bertie got soaked to the skin. By home time, Bertie was cold, wet, and sick and tired of being a slave. Still he'd done it — he'd made it to the end of the day and the reward was his!

"Ten pounds," he said to Royston in the cloakroom. "You owe me."

Royston checked his watch. "Actually the deal was until four o'clock," he reminded Bertie. "Which means we still have a good half an hour of slaving left."

He dumped his school bag at Bertie's feet.

"Carry that home, slave," he said. "And don't drop it."

Dirty Bertie

Bertie counted to ten. He wanted to throw the bag at Royston's big head. But he was so close to getting his hands on the money, he couldn't give up now.

"You coming, Bertie?" asked Darren.

Bertie sighed. "Royston wants me to carry his bag home," he said.

"Tell him to carry his own bag!" said Eugene.

"I can't, not until four o'clock!"

Darren and Eugene shook their heads. They couldn't believe Bertie was putting up with this!

They walked home together, taking the long way via Royston's house. Bertie had to lug Royston's bag as well as his own.

"It's so useful having a slave," Royston told Darren. "You really should try it some time."

Dirty Bertie

They stopped. They'd just turned into the alleyway that led to Royston's road but a giant puddle blocked the way. It was about a dozen paces across and looked at least ankle deep.

"We'll have to go round the other way," said Eugene.

"I don't think so," said Royston, glancing at his watch. "It'll take ages. We can get across."

"How?" asked Bertie.

"Simple. You'll just have to carry me," replied Royston.

Bertie stared at him. "You are kidding?" he said.

"Like I told you, that's what slaves are for," said Royston smugly. "I'm not getting my shoes wet."

"You're not really going to carry him?" said Darren.

"Tell him to get lost," advised Eugene.

Bertie looked at the wide brown puddle, then at Royston waiting to be carried across like royalty. All day he'd had to put up with that goofy face grinning at him. Well, no more, thought Bertie. There was only so much a person could take – even for a worm farm.

Royston climbed on to his back.

"Comfortable, your lordship?" said Bertie.

"Yes, and don't forget my bag," said Royston. "Come on, slave, giddy up!"

Bertie waded into the brown puddle, with Royston's bag in one hand. The water was so deep it sloshed over his shoes and soaked his socks. Halfway across he suddenly came to a halt.

"I didn't say stop!" shrieked Royston. "KEEP GOING!"

Bertie shook his head. "Ten pounds," he said. "By your watch, time's up, so hand it over."

"MOVE, SLAVE!" ordered Royston, digging his heels into Bertie's ribs.

Bertie didn't budge. "It's your last chance," he warned Royston.

"Don't answer back, and call me master!" shouted Royston, whacking Bertie on the shoulder.

That did it. Bertie let go of Royston's legs.

"ARGHHH! I'M ALL WET!" Royston howled, landing on his back. "HELP ME UP, YOU STUPID SLAVE!"

Royston raised a hand, which Bertie ignored. He dropped Royston's bag in the puddle with a splash.

"UGH! YOU… YOU…" cried Royston.

Bertie left Royston kicking his legs like a beetle on its back and returned to his friends.

"I think you can say goodbye to that ten pounds," said Eugene.

Bertie shrugged. "I know … but I've waited all day to do that and it was worth every penny!"

Royston scrambled to his feet and squelched to the other side of the puddle.

He turned back, waved his fists and

yelled, "I HATE YOU!"

Bertie bowed low. "And the same to you, your highness," he said.